THE FOX
& THE MOON

Inigo, Oriana,
Henry & Esther

First published in the United Kingdom in 2007 by Ragged Bears Publishing Limited,
Milborne Wick, Sherborne, Dorset DT9 4PW
www.raggedbears.co.uk

Distributed by Ragged Bears Distribution, a division of Publishers Group UK
8 the Arena, Mollison Avenue, Enfield, Middlesex EN3 7NL. Tel: 020 8804 0400

Text and illustrations copyright © 2007 Liz Graham-Yooll
The moral rights of the author and illustrator
of this work have been asserted

ALL RIGHTS RESERVED

A CIP record of this book is available from the British Library

ISBN 978 1 85714 374 4

Printed in China

THE FOX
& THE MOON

~ LIZ GRAHAM-YOOLL ~

RAGGED BEARS

Milborne Wick, Dorset

A handsome town fox woke up from his nap.
He yawned and he said, 'It's time for a snack.'

On that late autumn night, he wandered the streets,
looking for discarded food and any good treats.

He sniffed the cold air with his sharp little nose,
'What a good smell,' he said, 'I'd like one of those!'

He traced it to a yard, with a restaurant beside,
and saw a huge dustbin, with his dinner inside.

It was quiet and dark, but the container was large,
'Now how do I get in there?' he asked with a bark.

He circled around and sniffed the tall can.
'If I want to get in there, I must think of a plan.'

He had seen a large box, which he nosed to the side.
From this, he could leap to look down inside.

There were sweet and sour ribs,
still nice and hot.
'Yumm! I'd like to get those!'
he cried from the top.

BANG! A door slammed! This was such a huge fright
that he wobbled and toppled and vanished from sight.

He tried hard to escape, but it was ever in vain,
despite leaping and jumping again and again.

He awoke in the morning, to an ominous sound.
A truck was approaching and shaking the ground.

Big metal arms lifted the can in the air
and tipped the fox out, to his deepest despair.

The truck rattled away, past houses and fields,
along small country roads, to the big dump in the hills.

It shuddered to a stop, and tossed everything out
including the fox, who had been well bumped about.

'Hey!' cried a man. 'It's a fox. Look! Just there.'
And he chased the fox every which way and where.

He chased him and chased him, towards the dark woods.
'Help! Help!' yelped the fox, running as fast as he could.

'Thank goodness,' he gasped, 'that man's out of range.'
But, lost in the woods, he found it dark and so strange.

'This place is so scary,' he said, watching the shadows,
which crept over the ground and ate up the hollows.

'Why is it so dark, with not even a glow?
Where is the food that the people throw?'

But he was too tired to think, so he snuggled right down,
to fall deeply asleep, and then he dreamed of his town.

And he dreamed of a vixen, who sat right beside him.
She was pretty and dainty. She asked him a question.

'Where do you come from?' and she gave him a lick.
It came as a shock – he was up quick as quick!

'Hooray! I'm not dreaming,' he said, feeling bright.
'But where are the lamps to light the dark night?'

The vixen was puzzled, 'You must mean the moon.'
'Is that a light?' asked the fox. 'Whatever it is, turn it on soon.'

'And I'm so hungry,' he moaned, 'I could eat a horse!
I'd like chicken and pizza. And chips, of course.'

She went off for a second, then came smartly back,
carrying a dead mouse for his late evening snack.

'Ugh! How disgusting,' he cried. 'Please take it away.'
She said, 'I'll eat it myself, if you go on in this way.'

'Well, couldn't you toast it or dose it with ketchup?
'It looks horrible,' he sighed, but he still ate it up.

She taught him to hunt for food, day after day
and catch the poor hens, who were not put away.

He learned to eat roots, worms and gobble up mice,
until one fine day, he declared, 'This life is so nice!'

Night after night, they saw the moon wax and wane.
It grew from a sliver, until it was round once again.

Then they danced by the light of the full golden moon
and lived forever, together, from that late afternoon.

Other Ragged Bears books
that you might enjoy!

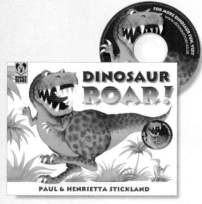

ISBN 1 85714 367 1
£6.99 • PB & CD

ISBN 978 1 85714 371 3
£4.99 • PB

ISBN 1 85714 217 9
£4.99 • PB

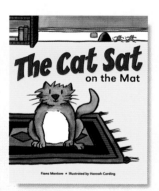

ISBN 978 1 85714 373 7
£4.99 • PB

ISBN 1 85714 276 4
£4.99 • PB

**Available from our website www.raggedbears.co.uk
or telephone 01963 34300 to be sent a full catalogue.**